GHOST IN A GOLDFISH BOWL

MICHÈLE BROWN
Illustrated by Guy Parker-Rees

CollinsChildren'sBooks
An Imprint of HarperCollinsPublishers

First published in Great Britain by
CollinsChildren'sBooks 1996

1 3 5 7 9 8 6 4 2

CollinsChildren'sBooks is an imprint of
HarperCollins*Publishers* Ltd,
77-85 Fulham Palace Road,
Hammersmith, London W6 8JB

Text copyright © Michele Brown 1996
Illustrations copyright © Guy Parker-Rees 1996

The author and illustrator assert the moral right to be
identified as the author and illustrator of the work.

Printed and bound in Great Britain by
Caledonian International Book Manufacturing Ltd, Glasgow G64

HB 0 00 185652 9
PB 0 00 675177 6

GHOST IN A GOLDFISH BOWL

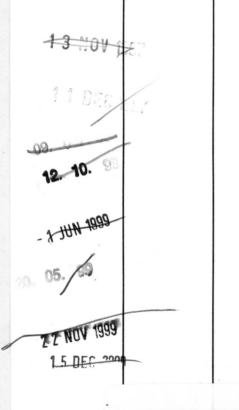

CHAPTER 1

Sally Smith was seven, very small and very sensible. Her mum always said that Sally was no trouble.

Sally had a lovely mum. She had a lovely dad, a lovely home and a lovely room of her own, right at the top of the house.

But there was one thing that Sally didn't have. She didn't have a pet. She really, really, really wanted a pet more than anything in the whole wide world.

Sally wanted a pet to be friends with...

A pet to have fun with...

A pet to sleep in her room, at the end of her bed.

"Pets are too much work," said Dad, who was always busy.

"Pets are too much fuss and bother," said Mum, who had more than enough to do already.

Sally's best friend was Tilly Thomas. At school, Sally told Tilly that Mum and Dad wouldn't let her have a pet.

"You could ask for a baby brother instead?" said Tilly.

This made them both start to giggle.

"What are you two girls giggling about?" said their teacher, Mrs Amos. "Please be sensible."

Sally and Tilly sat up straight and put on serious faces.

"Now," said Mrs Amos, "I want to remind you all about our visit to the Tower of London. Please be sure to bring in your money by the end of this week."

Sally was sure she would remember. She was saving up, keeping her money safely and sensibly. The money was in a goldfish bowl in her room. She *had* been going to use the goldfish bowl for a goldfish.

But that was before Mum and Dad had said, "Definitely no pets!"

Chapter 2

Sally had a dream that night.

It was a funny dream about owning a green parrot. Sally was trying to teach the parrot to talk.

First the parrot learnt to say, "Pretty Polly". Then it perched on Sally's shoulder and nibbled her ear with its beak.

"Excuse me!" said Sally crossly.

"Excuse me! Excuse me! Excuse me!" repeated the parrot. It spoke so loudly that Sally woke up.

It was the middle of the night and she was wide awake. She wasn't dreaming any more but she could still hear someone shouting.

"Excuse me! Excuse me! Excuse me!"

Then the same voice called out,
"Hello! Coo-ee! Is anybody there?"

Sally sat up and opened her eyes
very wide. Where was the voice
coming from?

It was really dark, but in the corner of the room, Sally could see the goldfish bowl. It was bright and white and… GLOWING!

The voice was coming from inside the goldfish bowl.

Sally crept out of bed. Slowly and bravely she tiptoed across the room. She peered down into the glowing goldfish bowl.

Looking up at her was a beaming round face.

"Oh boy, am I glad to see you," said the face. "Can you help me out of here. I just dropped in for a little snooze and now I seem to be stuck."

"Who are you?" whispered Sally.

"I'm a ghost, of course," said the face. "Isn't it obvious?"

Sally had never seen a ghost. She hadn't really thought about ghosts, she was far too sensible for that. She had certainly never expected to find a ghost stuck inside her goldfish bowl. Sally didn't know what to say.

"Please don't just stand there," said the jolly white face. "Be an angel and help me out. Just grab hold of a bit of me and pull and pull and pull and PULL!"

Sally did just that. She pulled and pulled and pulled and PULLED! Then suddenly, CRASH! BANG! FLUMP! The ghost popped out of the bowl with a whoosh and Sally fell over backwards, on to the floor.

"Tee hee! I'm free!" sang the ghost. "Oh boy, it was uncomfortable in there," he said. "It was like sitting on a pebbly beach."

"That's because you were squashed in on top of my pocket money," said Sally, as she scrambled back on to her feet. "I'm saving for our class outing to the Tower of London. The goldfish bowl is my money box."

The ghost gave a big beaming smile. "So that's what the trouble was," he said. "A goldfish bowl is cosy for a ghost, but not a goldfish bowl full of money. Would you be kind enough to remind me of that. I'm sure to forget about it. My memory is like a sieve. Nothing stays in it. Sometimes I even forget my own name."

Then he went floating round the
room singing, "Tee hee! Tee Hee!
I'm a ghost and I'm free!"

"Well I know *my* name - it's
Sally," said Sally.

"That's a nice name," said the
ghost. "I'm sure we're going to be
very good friends, Sally."

"What's your name?" asked Sally.
The ghost stopped floating
about. He looked puzzled. He
scratched the top of his head. Then
he went just a little bit pink.

"Oh dear," he said. "I do believe
I've quite forgotten."
Sally thought this was very funny.
"I shall call you Ghost," she said.

"You won't forget that. I'm very glad we're going to be friends. Now I must go back to sleep, or I'll be tired in the morning."

Sally really was *extremely* sensible.

Chapter 3

When Sally woke up the next morning, the sun was shining. She looked round but she couldn't see the ghost anywhere.

"Oh dear," thought Sally sadly.
"He's left without saying goodbye."
Then she heard a jolly voice
calling out, "Coo-ee! Sally, it's me."

The voice seemed to be coming
from the end of the bed.

Sally stared hard, but she still
couldn't see the ghost no matter
how wide she opened her eyes.

"Why can't I see you any more?" she asked.

"Because it's light," said the ghost. "You can only see me in the dark. I'm a ghost who glows in the dark!"

Next she heard him calling "Coo-ee! Sally! Can you find me?"

This time the voice seemed to come from *underneath* the bed.

Sally leant over the side of the bed and looked into the dark space underneath. Two large eyes were twinkling at her.

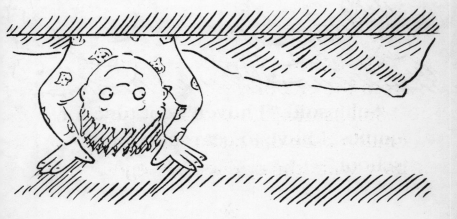

"Peep-bo!" shouted the ghost. "I love playing hide-and-seek, don't you?"

Sally said, "I haven't got time for games. I have to get ready for school."

When Sally went downstairs for breakfast, she could feel the ghost floating along, right behind her.

"What *would* Mum and Dad say if they knew my secret?" she thought.

Mum and Dad were sitting in the kitchen, drinking mugs of tea. They were both still half asleep. They were definitely not very good at getting up in the mornings. At breakfast time they always said to Sally, "We need peace and quiet."

But the ghost didn't feel like peace and quiet at all. He was ready for some fun.

Sally saw the door of the cupboard under the sink open. A voice from inside called out, "Psst! Let's play hide-and-seek! Coo-ee! Bet you can't find me."

"Did someone say something?" asked Dad, looking up from his mug of tea.

Sally jumped up to shut the cupboard door. But it was too late. The ghost had got away.

A few seconds later the lid of the
rubbish bin flew open with a bang.
"What on *earth* was that?" asked
Mum.

"YUK!" said the ghost, rather too
loudly. "I'm not hiding in there, it's
disgusting."
The lid of the rubbish bin banged
down again.

Dad looked amazed. "I must be hearing things," he said, shaking his head. "I think I need a holiday." He took a big gulp of tea.

Then Sally saw the fridge door swing open.

Before Mum and Dad could spot what was going on, Sally rushed over to the fridge and said, "I must get something for my lunchbox."

She stuck her head right inside
the fridge and whispered crossly,
"Stop that, at once."

Too late! The ghost was out of
the fridge and into the freezer.

A voice shouted "Yummee! My
favourite!"

A tub of vanilla ice cream
whizzed through the air.

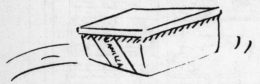

Mum and Dad stared at it with
their mouths open.

Sally couldn't see the ghost but she knew what he was doing. She ran across the kitchen and grabbed the tub just as it reached the table.

"I'm sorry, it just flew out of my fingers," she said. She quickly put the ice cream back in the freezer.

Mum looked astonished. "I must be seeing things," she said, shaking her head. "I need a holiday too." She took a big gulp of *her* tea.

Chapter 4

"You really must try to be sensible," Sally told the ghost as they went to school.

The ghost was holding on to her school-bag. Sally could feel him there, but nobody could see him.

"Mum and Dad said 'definitely no pets.' If they find out about you they'll say 'definitely no ghosts' as well!"

"Is it as much fun at school as it is in your house?" asked the ghost happily. "Do they have ice cream at school? Vanilla ice cream is my favourite. It looks just like me – soft, white and sort of fluffy. And it tastes yummee."

Sally sat down next to Tilly in the classroom.

"I'm in one of my tickly moods today," said the ghost in Sally's ear. "I'm looking for someone to tickle."

Sally felt him float away.

"Please be sensible," she called out to him.

Tilly thought Sally was speaking to her.

"I'm always sensible," said Tilly with a giggle.

Mrs Amos started to call out the register.

"Now for some fun," said the ghost, in Sally's other ear.

"Do *please* be quiet," begged Sally.

"What did you say Sally?" said Mrs Amos sharply.

"I just asked Tilly to be quiet," said Sally going red.

"Yes, do be quiet Tilly," said Mrs Amos.

Tilly gave Sally a very odd look indeed.

But Sally wasn't looking at Tilly. She was staring at a large feather floating up off the nature table and sailing straight towards Mrs Amos.

The feather tickled the end of the teacher's nose. Then it tickled her ear. Mrs Amos looked up. She rubbed her nose. She scratched her ear. The feather hid behind her head where Mrs Amos couldn't see it. As soon as she looked down again the feather was back, tickling her nose.

This time Mrs Amos did see it.
She tried to catch it but the feather
flew straight up to the ceiling.

"Why is that feather blowing
about?" asked Mrs Amos. "There
must be a draught. Someone please
make sure the door is closed
properly."

Sally got up and tried to grab the feather away from the ghost. But however high she stretched the feather stayed just out of reach.

"Sit down Sally," ordered Mrs Amos. "Take no notice, it will soon fall down."

But the feather *didn't* fall down. It started to dance round the room. It tickled the noses of all the children. Everyone started to sneeze. Everyone started to laugh.

"Stop! Stop!" shouted Sally. She was shouting at the ghost, but everyone thought she was shouting at the feather. *That* made them laugh even more.

"I thought I told you to sit down Sally," said Mrs Amos. "Be quiet *everybody*. Settle down."

But none of the children could stop laughing. There was chaos in the classroom until, at last, the feather floated down, back on to the nature table.

A voice chuckled in Sally's ear, "Well, that was good fun, wasn't it?"
"Oh dear," said Sally.

"Any more nonsense like that and nobody will be going to the Tower of London," said Mrs Amos, in her strictest voice. "Sally Smith, you were the worst. I don't know what's come over you. You are usually so *sensible*."

When they got home after school, Sally and the ghost were tired out.

"It's hard work keeping a secret all day," said Sally.

"Keeping secrets makes me hungry," said the ghost. "I'd love some yummee ice cream."

"Well I'm far too tired to get some for you," said Sally. "I need a good sleep. But please remember, definitely no silly tricks tonight!"

Chapter 5

The next morning, before they set off for school, Sally took the ghost into the cupboard under the stairs. It was nice and dark in there. Sally could see the ghost glowing clearly.

"You must promise to be very
sensible today," she said sternly.
"Any more trouble and Mrs Amos
will be very cross. Then none of the
class will be allowed to go to the
Tower of London.

The ghost looked very sorry.

"I mean to be good," he said, "but
I get over-excited when I'm playing,
and I forget."

The ghost made a big effort to be extra good at school.

So did Sally. She put up her hand for all the questions. She didn't giggle at a single one of Tilly's silly jokes.

"You're not much fun today," said Tilly, in a fed-up voice.

When school ended Mrs Amos said, "That was much better Sally."

Sally gave a big sigh of relief. She wasn't going to miss the visit to the Tower of London after all.

That night she went to the goldfish bowl to count her money out, ready for the morning.

CATASTROPHE! It wasn't there!

"Where is it?" cried Sally.

"Where's what?" asked the ghost.

"My pocket money," said Sally.
"It's disappeared."

"It can't have disappeared," said
the ghost. "You must have put it
somewhere. Now think hard.
Where have you been? Let's play a
game of hide-and-seek and see if
we can find it?"

They searched high and they searched low.

The ghost floated up to the ceiling and peered into the lightshade.

Sally got on to her hands and knees and peered under the bed.

They looked inside the wardrobe. They looked on the bookshelf. They looked behind the chest of drawers. They even looked under the mattress. There was no sign of the money anywhere.

At last, Sally got into bed. She was feeling very unhappy indeed. "I'll have to tell Mum and Dad in the morning," she said. "They'll be furious."

"Don't worry Sally," said the ghost. "I have very good ideas. I'm sure I'll think of something. Just leave it to me." He floated off and tucked himself into the goldfish bowl to have a really good think.

He thought and thought... and thought and thought. But it was no use, he didn't have a single good idea. In fact he didn't have any ideas at all. Except for one.

"I think I'll have some of that yummee vanilla ice cream," he thought. "That will help me to think better."

He floated out of the room very quietly so as not to wake Sally. He floated down the stairs very quietly, so as not to wake Mum and Dad. He floated very quietly into the kitchen and over to the freezer.

Inside the freezer he found just what he was looking for. A big tub of his favourite vanilla ice cream.

First he put the tub of ice cream on the table. Next he took a big spoon out of the drawer. Then he opened the lid of the ice cream, closed his eyes and dipped the spoon into the tub.

"Yummee!" he chuckled. "This is going to be good."

"YUK!"

It wasn't ice cream at all. It was hard and tasted horrible. The ghost completely forgot his manners and spat the hard bits out.

When he opened his eyes he saw that there was no yummee vanilla ice cream in the tub. Instead there was money. Lots and lots of money. The ice-cream tub was FULL of money!

"Oh boy!" said the ghost to himself. "I think I've found Sally's pocket money. But how did it get into the ice-cream tub. It's a complete mystery."

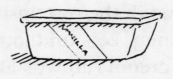

Chapter 6

Sally thought she was dreaming again. She could hear somebody calling out "Excuse me! Excuse me! Excuse me!"

Then she heard a voice saying, "Coo-ee! Sally, can you hear me?"

Sally woke up. She saw the ghost floating by her bed. He was glowing very brightly and there was a big smile on his face.

"What is it?" asked Sally sleepily.

"I've found your money," said the ghost excitedly. "I knew I could do it and I did." He put the ice-cream tub down on Sally's pillow.

"Ghost, you're brilliant!" said Sally. "But why is the money in the ice-cream tub?"

"I don't know. I found it in the freezer when I went to get some ice cream," explained the ghost. "But don't ask me how it got there. It's a complete mystery."

Sally thought hard for a while. Then she said. "Did you go down to the kitchen for ice cream the other night?"

"I might have done," said the ghost. "I can't really remember."

"And when you woke up the next morning, were you sleeping in the goldfish bowl?" asked Sally.

"I might have been," said the ghost. "I can't really remember."

"You are funny, Ghost" laughed
Sally. "Now I know what you did."
"Do you?" said the ghost.

"You took the money out of the
goldfish bowl so that it would be
nice and comfortable to sleep in."
"Did I?" said the ghost.

"Then you took the money with you when you went downstairs for some ice cream."

"Did I?" said the ghost.

"And then you finished up all the ice cream and put the money in the empty ice-cream tub," said Sally.

"WHY YES, SO I DID!" shouted the ghost.

"You really *do* have a bad memory, don't you," laughed Sally.

"I've got a memory like a goldfish," said the ghost, shaking his head sadly. "Please don't be cross with me."

But Sally wasn't cross at all. She thought the ghost was very funny when he forgot things. She thought he was very funny when he played hide-and-seek. She thought he was even funnier when he wanted to tickle people. She thought he was much, much more fun than any pet could possibly be.

"I'm going to tell Mum and Dad that I don't want a pet any more," Sally said. "It's much nicer being friends with a ghost."

"We'll have a lovely time together," said the ghost.

"You can play lots of silly tricks," said Sally.

"We can eat lots and lots of yummee ice cream," said the ghost.

"And you can sleep on the end of my bed, just like a pet," said Sally. "It's much more sensible than sleeping in a goldfish bowl."

"I *quite* agree," said the ghost.